The Magic School Bus Rides Again

Carlos Gets the Sneezes

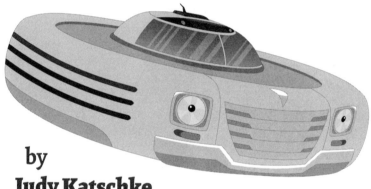

by
Judy Katschke

BRANCHES
SCHOLASTIC INC.

Ms. Frizzle's Class

Jyoti

Arnold

Ralphie

Wanda

Keesha

Dorothy Ann

Carlos

Tim

TABLE OF CONTENTS

© 2018 Scholastic Inc.
Based on the television series *The Magic School Bus: Rides Again*.
© 2017 MSB Productions, Inc.
Based on the *Magic School Bus*® series © Joanna Cole and Bruce Degen.
All rights reserved.

Published by Scholastic Inc., *Publishers since 1920*.
SCHOLASTIC, THE MAGIC SCHOOL BUS, BRANCHES, and logos are trademarks and/or registered trademarks of Scholastic Inc. All rights reserved.

The publisher does not have any control over and does not assume any responsibility for author or third-party websites or their content.

Library of Congress Cataloging-in-Publication Data available

ISBN 978-1-338-19446-3 (paperback) / ISBN 978-1-338-23212-7 (hardcover)

10 9 8 7 6 5 4 3 2 1   18 19 20 21 22
Printed in China   38

First edition, April 2018
Book design by Jessica Meltzer
Edited by Marisa Polansky

CHAPTER 1

OUT OF THE BOX!

For Carlos only,'" Dorothy Ann read out loud. "'Do not touch. Signed, Wanda.'"

Dorothy Ann, Jyoti, Ralphie, Keesha, Tim, and Arnold stood around a box covered by a blanket. Ralphie reached for the blanket.

"I wonder what's in it?" he said.

1

"'PS,'" Dorothy Ann read on. "'That means you, Ralphie!'"

"Oh, man!" Ralphie groaned.

Carlos was the only one of Ms. Frizzle's students who was allowed to open the mysterious package, but he wasn't around. So everyone else began taking wild guesses about what was inside the box.

As usual, Tim had comics on the brain. "Maybe it's a rare copy of a *Tiger-antula* comic," he guessed.

"Or a pizza fountain!" Ralphie declared. The one thing Ralphie loved more than surprises was pizza!

"Or safety goggles!" Arnold said.

Safety goggles? The class stared at Arnold. "What?" Arnold shrugged. "It's a sensible gift."

Just then, Carlos walked into the classroom.

"Carlos, check it out," Keesha said. "Wanda left this for you."

Carlos's eyes lit up when he saw the covered box. He knew exactly what was inside. "Yes! Finally!" he cheered. "You guys are going to love this. Ready?"

Dorothy, Jyoti, Ralphie, Keesha, Tim, and Arnold leaned in for the big reveal . . .

"Ta-daaa!" Carlos sang. He yanked off the cloth to reveal a cage. An empty cage!

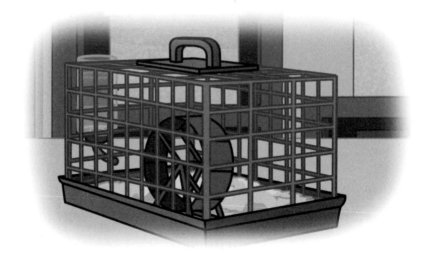

"Oh, just what I've always wanted. An empty cage," joked Ralphie.

"Where is she?" Carlos asked.

"Who?" the others asked.

"Ratney. That's who," said Wanda. She entered the classroom holding something wrapped in a blanket. It was a little white rat!

"Ratney got out and into the yard, but I found her," Wanda explained. "Say, hi, Ratney!"

5

Arnold gulped when he saw Ratney. He was always worrying about lots of things. Now he had one more thing to worry about—a rat!

"Ratney?" Arnold asked. "As in an actual rat?"

"Looks like it, Arnold," Keesha said with a smile. "And it's got a face only Carlos could love!"

Carlos lifted Ratney out of the fluffy blanket. "Say hello to our new class pet!" he said.

CHAPTER 2

SNEEZE AND
THANK YOU

The kids couldn't believe their eyes. Class pets were usually gerbils, hamsters, or funny little lizards named Liz, but a *rat*?

"Carlos," Dorothy Ann asked, "did you get permission from Principal Ruhle to keep her?"

"Not yet," Carlos said, "but I wrote an awesome speech, so there's no way he'll say no."

Ralphie got an idea.

"Pretend I'm Mr. Ruhle," Ralphie said, "and convince me to let you keep a rat in the classroom."

Carlos lifted Ratney close to his face. "Well, Mr. Ruhle," he practiced, "to begin with, I . . . I . . . ah-chooooo!"

Ratney blinked. Carlos's sneeze was followed by another. And another. And another!

"We're all going to get sick!" Arnold cried. He grabbed a blanket off the shelf and tossed it over his head. "Hide me!"

Arnold wasn't the only student who was worried. Carlos was worried about Ratney.

"Aw, man," Carlos groaned. "How can I make a pitch for Ratney if I'm . . . I'm . . . aaaa-choooo . . . sick!"

Wanda held out tissues. Carlos grabbed one and blew his nose with a loud HONK!

"You can't make your case like that, Carlos," Tim insisted. "You'll make Mr. Ruhle sick, too, and he won't be happy about that."

"Tim's right," Jyoti agreed. "You have to get rid of your cold first."

Carlos shook his head. He couldn't wait until he stopped sneezing. He needed to get permission to keep Ratney or else!

"I have to talk to Mr. Ruhle today," Carlos insisted, "or we have to take Ratney to the . . . the . . . ah-choooo!"

"He means the shelter," Wanda **translated**.

The sound of Carlos's sneezes filled the classroom. The kids heard another sound. The sound got louder and louder. Suddenly, a mysterious figure walked in wearing a space suit.

The mysterious visitor removed the heavy helmet. It was their teacher, Ms. Frizzle!

"Ms. Frizzle, why are you wearing that?" Keesha asked.

"Because where we're going is not exactly dress-friendly," Ms. Frizzle replied.

"Uh-oh," Arnold said, still under the blanket. "I smell a field trip."

"Indeed you do, Arnold," Ms. Frizzle said. "We'll see what's going on inside Carlos before you can say 'gesundheit.'"

"That's it!" Wanda said. "We'll go inside your nose, Carlos."

"We'll help your **immune system** fight those nasty germs and get rid of your cold," Tim said. "Then you can talk to Mr. Ruhle about Ratney."

"Class, to the bus!" shouted Ms. Frizzle.

"We'll be in touch, Carlos," Ms. Frizzle promised Carlos. She scanned Carlos's body for his **biometrics**. Next, she projected a full diagram of his body on the blackboard.

Carlos had never seen himself inside out before. "Wow," he exclaimed. "Is that me?"

"Yes, it is," Ms. Frizzle said. She turned to their class pet lizard. "Liz, you're on tissue patrol, to help Carlos sneeze with ease."

Liz gave a little salute and handed Carlos a tissue. While Carlos blew his nose, Ms. Frizzle blew out of the school to the Magic School Bus.

CHAPTER 3

THE NOSE KNOWS

Ms. Frizzle's Magic School Bus had once belonged to her big sis, Professor Frizzle. It could change into anything Ms. Frizzle needed to teach her lesson. Today's lesson was Carlos's immune system!

"All aboard the Immune Express!" Ms. Frizzle called. She waited until everyone was aboard. Then—WHOOSH—the door slammed shut.

Everyone held on tight as the bus began to spin and shrink. It kept shrinking until it was tiny enough to zoom through their classroom window.

"The bus is making its final approach," Ms. Frizzle reported through a microphone. "Carlos, prepare nostril for entry."

Carlos turned to Ratney, who was snuggled in her blanket. "I'm doing this for you, Ratney," he said. "I hope you appreciate it."

Ratney scratched at her fur. After another big sneeze, Carlos braced for impact.

"Around his toes—" Ms. Frizzle said.

The mosquito-sized bus zipped around and around Carlos's ankles.

"And up his nose it goes!"

The Magic School Bus shot up Carlos's nostril. The kids gazed out the windows to see a world of goopy nose hairs and gobs of snot.

"Goop alert!" Ralphie cried.

"What are those things?" Wanda asked.

"Sit back, relax, and enjoy," Ms. Frizzle told the kids. "On your left are Carlos's nose hairs. They are the first line of defense against incoming germs, unwanted particles, and tiny buses."

The kids heard a loud grinding noise. It sounded like the bus tires were spinning, but the bus wasn't moving.

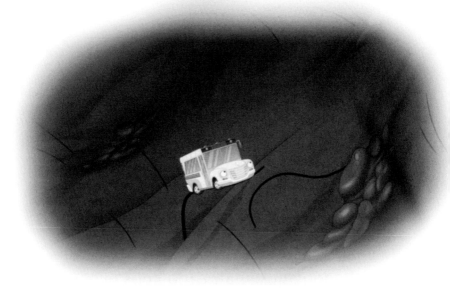

"We're stuck on a nose hair!" Arnold cried.

Another worried face popped up on the bus's monitor. It was Carlos's. "Ms. Frizzle?" he said. "I feel another sneeze coming on."

Ms. Frizzle wasn't worried. A huge sneeze might be just what the doctor ordered!

"Seat belts, everyone!" Ms. Frizzle called out.

"Ah-chooooo!" Carlos sneezed. It was his biggest sneeze yet. It was big enough to rocket the bus out of the nose hair!

Everyone held on tight as The Magic School Bus shot around like a pinball.

"What's happening, Ms. Frizzle?" Wanda asked.

"Exactly what's supposed to happen when something's in your nose that doesn't belong," Ms. Frizzle explained. "We're being blown away!"

Blown away? That's not what Wanda wanted to hear!

"We can't leave, Ms. Frizzle," Wanda said. "We have to help Carlos!"

"And so we will, Wanda," Ms. Frizzle said with a smile. She reached out and flipped a switch. A clawlike gadget rose from the roof of the bus. It grabbed a nose hair, stretched it way back like a slingshot, and then let it go with a BOOOINNG!

"Ahhhhhhh!" the kids screamed.

The Magic School Bus zoomed up Carlos's nose into total darkness.

CHAPTER 4

BODY BATTLE

Where are we, Ms. Frizzle?" Tim asked. Outside The Magic School Bus were round white discs.

"We're in Carlos's bloodstream!" Ms. Frizzle said. She turned around in the driver's seat. "Okay, class. Look for a cold virus. It's the thing that makes you sick."

"I would," Wanda said. "If I had any clue what I was looking for."

As always, Dorothy Ann had the answer right at her fingertips. She swiped her tablet and said, "According to my research, there are over two hundred cold-causing viruses!"

Dorothy Ann flipped around her tablet to show the most common one: a purple blob with hairy-looking things sticking out of it!

"That virus is having one seriously bad hair day!" Ralphie joked.

"And it will have an even worse day if Carlos's **white blood cells** find it," Ms. Frizzle said.

The kids looked out to see what Ms. Frizzle meant. *Whoa!* An army of the white blood cells was surrounding their bus!

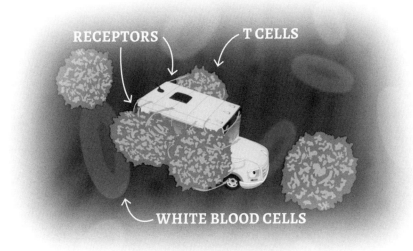

RECEPTORS

T CELLS

WHITE BLOOD CELLS

"You mean like those?" Tim asked.

Different blobs popped out of the cells. They had wavy tentacles called receptors that were reaching for the bus!

"Yikes!" Keesha gasped. "What are they?"

"**T cells**," Ms. Frizzle replied. "They help the white blood cells hunt down and destroy the **invaders**."

"Uh-oh." Arnold gulped. "What if they think we're the invaders?"

"I'd say we're about to find out," Ralphie said.

WHAP! The T cells glued themselves onto the bus.

"We're under attack!" Ralphie shouted.

"AHHHHHH!" Everyone screamed as the T cells tipped the Magic School Bus upside down.

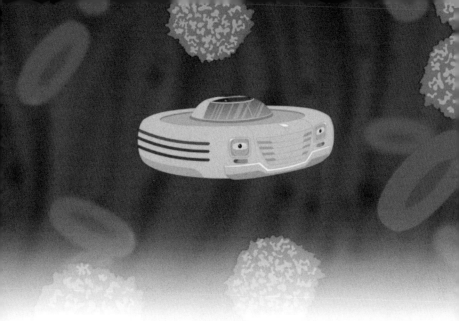

CHAPTER 5

READY FOR RATNEY

Whoooooaaa!" the kids shouted as they slipped and slid toward the front of the bus.

On the way, Ralphie bumped into a button. POOF! The Magic School Bus changed into a cell shaped like a disc. They looked just like Carlos's other cells. Suddenly, the T cells let go of the bus and floated away!

"Well done, Ralphie," Ms. Frizzle declared.
"You hit the Regular-Cell-a-Nator."

"The Regular-Cell-a-Nator?" the kids asked.

"Yeah, I named it myself," joked Ms. Frizzle.
"Now we look just like one of Carlos's normal,
everyday cells," Ms. Frizzle explained.

"So we don't have to worry about Carlos's
immune system destroying us?" Ralphie asked.

Ms. Frizzle nodded, and said, "It also means
that Carlos's immune system is working A-OK!"

A-OK was great news for Carlos. But Dorothy Ann was confused. "We haven't seen any cold viruses yet," she said.

"So I don't have a cold?" Carlos asked.

"It doesn't look like it," Ms. Frizzle said.

"All systems normal, Carlos," Dorothy Ann said as she read his results. "Body temperature. Check. Blood pressure. Check."

Carlos smiled at the great news. All systems normal meant all systems go for Ratney!

"Awesome!" Carlos cheered. "So, if I can't make Mr. Ruhle sick, I'll go talk to him now."

Carlos grabbed Ratney's cage. "Come on, Ratney," he said, "and don't forget to smile!"

Carlos walked excitedly to Principal Ruhle's office. He held Ratney's cage as he practiced his lines.

"And so you see, Mr. Ruhle, " Carlos said to himself, "Ratney is a really awesome rat. Look at her. So adorable!"

Mr. Ruhle's secretary sat outside his office. "Mr. Ruhle will see you now, Carlos," she said.

"Great!" Carlos said. But as he stepped toward Mr. Ruhle's office his nose began to tickle. Then—

"Ah-choooooooo!"

Ratney's cage bounced in and out of Carlos's hands as he sneezed and sneezed!

"Carlos, are you okay?" the secretary asked. Carlos tried to answer. All that came out of his mouth was, "Ah-choo ah-choo ah-choo ah-choo ah-choo!"

"We should probably postpone your appointment, Carlos," the secretary said, "until you're feeling better."

Rats! Carlos couldn't leave Mr. Ruhle's office. Not without showing him Ratney!

"No, it's really important," Carlos said, "I need to—ah-choo ah-choo ah-choo ah-choo!"

The secretary handed Carlos a tissue. "Another time then," she said. But Carlos needed more than a tissue. He needed another chance with Mr. Ruhle!

"No!" Carlos pleaded. "I—ah-choo ah-choo!"

The big sneeze blew Carlos and Ratney through the door. They were out in the hall—and out of luck!

CHAPTER 6

BOOGER BRIGADE

Y̲ou guys said I don't have a cold," Carlos said to the screen. "So how come my eyes are still watering and I'm still—ah-choo—sneezing?"

The class looked out the window. Carlos's cells were attacking strange-looking particles, and their bus was in the middle of it!

"Your immune system is under attack, Carlos," Wanda told him.

"Again?" Arnold groaned.

"What are those particles, and why are Carlos's white blood cells attacking them?" asked Wanda.

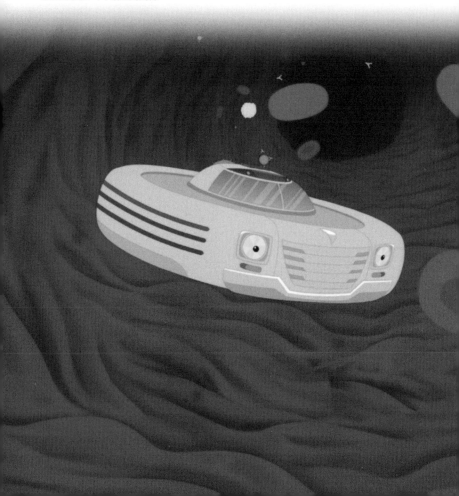

Dorothy Ann turned back to her tablet.

"I've gone through every single cold virus." She sighed. "And nothing matches!"

The bus gave a sudden jolt.

"Hang tight!" Jyoti called out. "We're on the move again!"

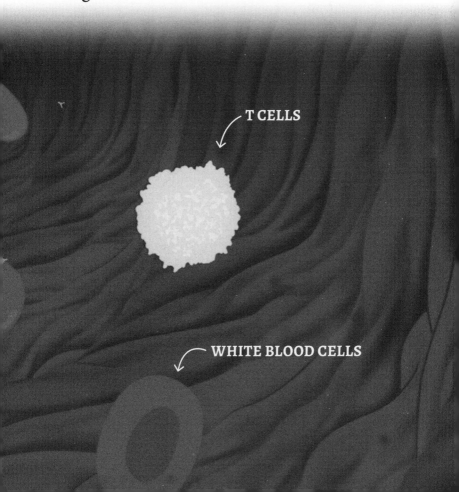

T CELLS

WHITE BLOOD CELLS

The bus cruised through a tunnel. It was jam-packed with liquid and a tangle of webby **fibers**.

"We're now entering the mucous membrane," Ms. Frizzle announced, "also known as Booger Boulevard."

"Also known as gross," Arnold muttered.

The particles crashed into the cells. The cells popped open and began to spray.

"What's that stuff?" Tim asked.

"According to my research," Dorothy Ann said, eyeing her tablet, "what the cells are spraying is called histamine."

"Histamine?" Ralpie asked.

"Histamine makes you sneeze so you get rid of the invaders," Dorothy Ann explained.

Just then, T cells began to carry the particles through Carlos's bloodstream.

"T cells to the rescue!" Ms. Frizzle declared. "Wahoo!"

"And the winner is," Ralphie announced, "Carlos's immune system by a nose hair!"

"Not so fast, Ralphie!" Wanda said. She pointed out the window to a flood of particles. "The bad guys are back! There are too many for the immune system to take away!"

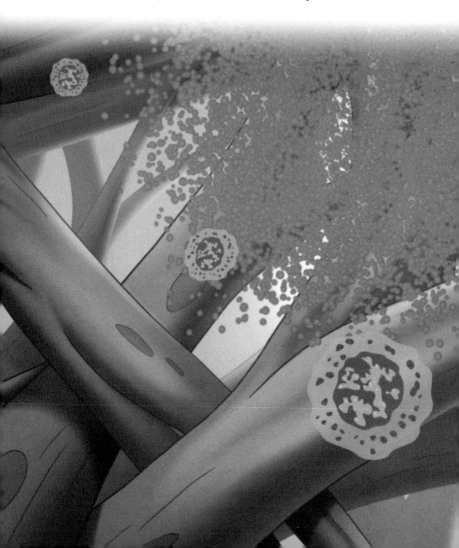

Soon, Booger Boulevard was bouncing with pesky particles. But the kids in Ms. Frizzle's class refused to let the invaders win.

"Time for action, you guys," Jyoti said. "We said we'd help Carlos, so let's do it!"

"Yeah!" Keesha said. "But how?"

The kids watched as a cell attacked a particle. This cell was special.

"Dorothy Ann," Wanda said, "what kind of cell is that?"

"According to my research," Dorothy Ann said, "that's called an **antibody**."

"Well, that antibody has an awesome weapon!" said Keesha.

"It looks like the immune system can tell who the bad guys are," Tim said, "by those marker things on them."

The class watched as the weapon on the antibody and the marker on the particle slid together like matching puzzle pieces.

"That's how the antibodies grab the invaders!" Dorothy Ann said.

"Let's help the T cells catch those particles and take them away," Jyoti said.

"How do we catch them?" Wanda asked. "We can't just grab them with our hands."

"I can design something to grab them," Jyoti said. "But first, I'll need to get a better look at those particles."

"They're moving around so fast!" Keesha said.

"Right," Jyoti agreed. "So to get what I need—"

"We have to catch one!" Wanda shouted.

CHAPTER 7

BLOW AWAY!

Keesha, Wanda, and Jyoti suited up. They put on wet suits with built-in jetpacks. Ms. Frizzle handed each girl a cone-shaped jar to catch particles. "Happy hunting, girls," she said.

Ms. Frizzle pulled a lever. The floor underneath them popped open. The girls dropped out of the bus and landed with a SPLAT in a pile of sticky mucus!

"Ewwww!" they said together.

They flipped a switch on their jets and blasted out of the mucus.

Jyoti eyed tons of floating particles. "Jars up," she declared, "We're going in!"

"Let's split up," Keesha suggested. "It'll be faster."

Keesha swam away from Jyoti and Wanda.

Ralphie looked out the window. "Uh-oh." Ralphie gulped. "What if Carlos's immune system thinks they're invaders, like it did with the bus?"

Suddenly, an army of T cells zoomed toward Jyoti and Wanda! They began surrounding them.

"We're under attack!" Jyoti exclaimed.

"They think we're the bad guys!" Wanda said.

Just then, a button started blinking on Wanda's belt. It looked just like the button from the bus.

"Jyoti!" Wanda called. "Hit your Regular-Cell-a-Nator!"

Wanda's and Jyoti's suits morphed to look like Carlos's cells.

"Nice!" Jyoti cheered.

The girls didn't look like invaders anymore, so the cells scattered away.

"Where's Keesha?" asked Wanda.

Then the girls heard her voice coming from far away.

"Come here, you pesky particles!" Keesha called.

She pushed through tangled fibers to chase after the floating particles.

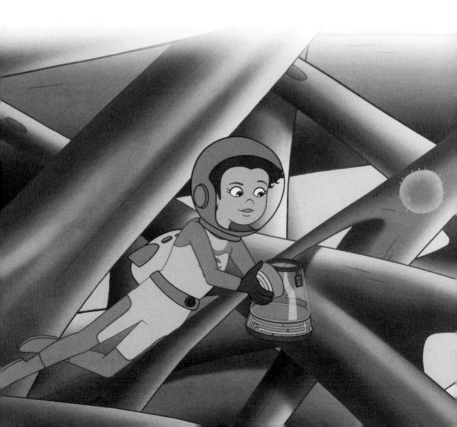

"Gotcha!" Keesha exclaimed.

She scooped a particle into her jar. Before she could twist on the lid—POOF! The light and fluffy particle popped out of the jar!

PARTICLE

"No, I don't gotcha." Keesha sighed.

She chased the particle, swooped it into the jar, and screwed the lid on fast!

Just then, a T cell found her. It grabbed her and dragged Keesha up through Carlos's nose.

"AAAAAAH,"Keesha yelled.

CHAPTER 8

HE'S GONNA BLOW!

Jyoti and Wanda heard Keesha's yell. They pushed through sticky mucus to find their friend dangling from the T cell!

"Hang on, Keesha!" Wanda called.

"I'm hanging!" Keesha called.

Wanda grabbed onto Keesha's legs and Jyoti grabbed Wanda's. A hurricane-force gust sent mucus pouring out of Carlos's nostril. The girls held on to a nose hair to keep from being blown out, too.

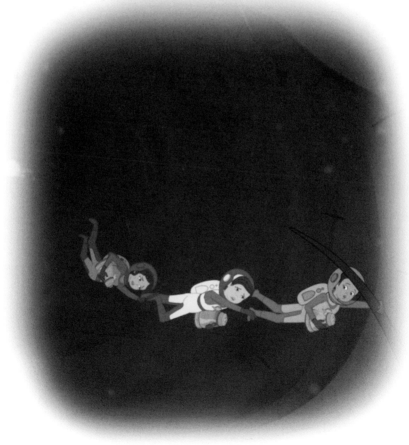

"Carlos must have sneezed!" said Jyoti.

"You think?" joked Keesha whose helmet was covered in mucus.

At least you held on to the particle, Keesha!" said Jyoti.

"Let's get out of here," said Keesha.

The girls headed to the bus. When they got inside, they placed the jar on a pedestal to be inspected.

"Good job, guys!" said Tim. "Now let's figure this thing out!"

Dorothy Ann scrolled her tablet for pictures of viruses and shook her head. "This particle doesn't match anything in my database," she said. "No cold. No flu. Nothing."

"So if Carlos isn't sick," Tim said, "how come he's still sneezing?"

I sneeze sometimes when I'm not sick," Arnold said. "My doctor says it's allergies."

"That's it!" said Ralphie. "Good job, Arn."

Dorothy Ann found allergy information on her tablet. "According to my research," she said, "an allergic reaction happens when your immune system attacks particles called allergens!"

"It tries to get rid of them, too!" Keesha said.

"Arnold," Wanda asked, "when you're allergic what does the doctor say to do?"

"He tells me to stay away from the stuff I'm allergic to," Arnold replied. "Then the sneezing and drippy eyes go away."

Wanda couldn't wait to share the news. She grabbed the microphone and shouted, "Attention, Carlos!"

Carlos was sitting on the classroom floor between towers of tissues. Ratney was curled up in his lap.

"Yeah?" Carlos sniffed.

"You're not sick, Carlos," Wanda told him. "You're allergic to something, and we need to know what it is."

"How do I find out?" Carlos asked.

"You were fine yesterday," Wanda said. "So find out what's different now from then. Get it?"

"Got it!" Carlos replied.

But while Carlos's nose kept running, time in his immune system was running out. The battle of the cells raged on, and the allergens were winning!

"Carlos still needs our help!" Keesha said.

CHAPTER 9

JAB AND GRAB

Carlos's allergens were out of control. The class had to do something to help. Jyoti and Tim had taken control of the bus's **3-D printer**.

"I've given the printer my allergy grabber design," said Jyoti. "As soon as it's finished printing, we'll have the perfect tool to give Carlos's immune system the help it needs!"

They studied a scan of the particle on the computer screen. A marker on the particle flashed on and off.

"Marker sync," the computer voice said. "Perfect match!"

Jyoti opened the printer and pulled out her latest invention: a grabber gadget with something extra. The end of the grabber matched markers on the allergens!

"Here's the plan," Jyoti said. "We grab the allergens with this and haul them away!"

"A grab-and-destroy mission," Ralphie said. "For Carlos!" The class cheered.

The kids dropped from the bus ready to take on the allergens.

Jyoti and her friends had hit their Regular-Cell-a-Nator so they matched Carlos's cells. They jabbed, grabbed, and dragged particles into a bag.

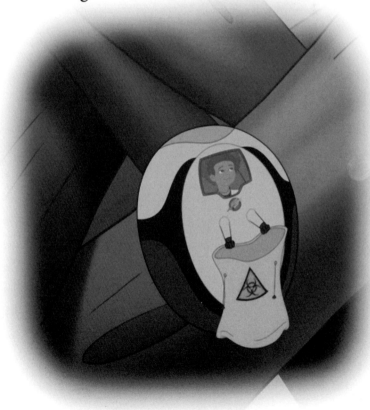

Suddenly—WHOOSH—a wall of allergens headed straight for them.

"Watch out!" said Tim. "Why are there so many allergens all of a sudden?"

"We can't stick around to find out!" yelled Jyoti.

The kids made it to the bus just in time. They watched as tons of allergens blew past the windows.

"What could be causing this?" asked Keesha.

Wanda had an idea. "Carlos!" she called. "What are you doing?"

Carlos's face flashed on the screen. "Koochy-koochy-koo!" he said, smiling.

Everyone traded puzzled looks.

Koochy-koochy-whaaa?

"Carlos, whatever you're doing right now," Wanda said, "that's what's been causing your allergies!"

"But I'm not doing anything," Carlos said. "I'm just petting Ratney's stomach. Koochy-koochy..."

Carlos stopped mid-sentence. His fingers froze over Ratney. The answer to his sneezing problem was right under his nose and in his lap!

"Arrgh!" Carlos cried. "I'm allergic to Ratney!"

CHAPTER 10

RAT-FREE

The kids made it back to the classroom to reunite with Carlos.

"I'm so sorry, Carlos," Wanda said.

Ms. Frizzle's class trip through Carlos's immune system had ended, but the hardest part was about to begin.

"I'm sorry, too," Carlos said as he sat next to Ratney's cage. "I guess we have to take Ratney to the shelter, right?"

Wanda nodded, and said, "They'll find a good home for her with someone who isn't allergic to her."

"I know it's for the best." Carlos sighed. "But I don't have to like it."

Wanda and Carlos walked together to the animal shelter. A woman who worked there greeted them.

"Sorry you can't keep Ratney, Carlos," the woman said. "We'll find the right home for her."

Saying good-bye was super hard. But as they walked back to school, Wanda noticed something neat.

"Guess what, Carlos?" Wanda said. "You haven't sneezed once since we gave Ratney back."

"You're right," Carlos said.

They walked past a garden, and Wanda stopped. "That's where I found Ratney this morning," she said, pointing to the flowers.

Carlos sniffed. He rubbed his watery eyes.

"It's okay to cry for Ratney," Wanda said.

Carlos shook his head. His eyes were watering, but he wasn't crying. He was about to say that to Wanda when—

"Ah-ah-ah-chooooooooo!"

Wanda stared at Carlos as he sneezed and sneezed. She looked from Carlos to the flowers. Then from the flowers to Carlos. *Hmmm.*

"I wonder," Wanda said. She plucked a flower and held it under Carlos's nose. "Sniff!" she said.

"Ah-choo-ah-choo-ah-choo-ah-choo!"

Carlos's sneezes came fast and furious.

"Carlos," Wanda said with a smile, "what if you're not allergic to Ratney?"

"Not allergic to Ratney?" Carlos asked between sneezes. "What else could be making me sneeze like this?"

"What if you're allergic to the pollen in this flower?" Wanda asked.

Carlos stared at the flower in Wanda's hand. "You mean maybe the pollen got stuck to Ratney's fur?" he asked.

"Only one way to find out!" said Wanda.

CHAPTER 11

CARLOS'S CELL-A-BRATION

Wanda and Carlos brought the flower back to the classroom. Dorothy Ann inspected it under the microscope.

"Do you know yet, Dorothy Ann?" Carlos asked. "How about now?"

"Don't rush me," she said. "We need to be sure the pollen from the flower matches the particle that attacked Carlos's immune system."

A blowup of the pollen particle and a blowup of the particle from Carlos's immune system appeared on the blackboard screen. They looked exactly alike. But were they? With a single swipe, Dorothy Ann merged the particles together.

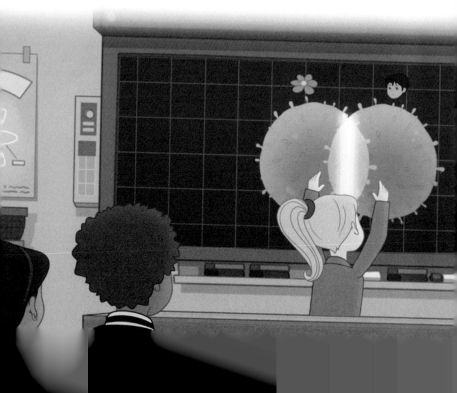

"It's a match!" Dorothy declared.

"Wahoo!" cheered the class.

Since Carlos wasn't allergic to Ratney, she could be their class pet!

"It's up to Principal Ruhle, Carlos," Ms. Frizzle said. "But we'd better guarantee our friend is pollen-free."

The kids knew what to do. First, they picked Ratney up from the shelter. Next, they treated her to a bubble bath and a stylin' blow-dry. Ratney was ready for Mr. Ruhle and her close-up!

"Say sneeze!" Carlos said as Ms. Frizzle took a photo.

Thanks to her makeover, Ratney looked picture-perfect. But the real test would come in the principal's office.

"Mr. Ruhle will see you now," the secretary said. Carlos entered the office. Carlos held Ratney as he opened the door. He was about to step into Mr. Ruhle's office when—

"Ah-choooo! Ah-chooo! Ah-chooo!"

Carlos held Ratney's cage as Mr. Ruhle sneezed and blew his nose. Wow. Who knew their principal would be allergic to rats?

"What are you going to do, Carlos?" the secretary asked.

Carlos smiled. He knew exactly what to do.

"I guess I'll have to take Ratney to another house," Carlos said. *"My house!"*

On the way home from school, Carlos passed the garden. "Nuh-uh," he said to Ratney. "I've got an even better home for you."

"Ratney," Carlos said, "I think this is the start of a beautiful and sneeze-free friendship."

GLOSSARY

3-D printer: a machine that prints a physical object

Antibody: a protein that your blood makes to stop an infection that has entered your body

Biometrics: the measurement of physical or behavioral characteristics in a body

Fiber: a thin strand of material

Immune system: the system that protects your body against disease and infection

Invader: an entity that has entered a place or situation in large numbers, usually with a negative effect

Mucous membrane: a lining in the body that produces mucous

T cell: a type of white blood cell that attacks different invaders in the immune system

Translated: changed from one language to another

White blood cell: a group of cells that help protect our bodies from sickness

Ask Professor Frizzle

I loved Ratney! Should I ask my parents for a pet rat?

 Rats can make excellent pets, but be sure to get one that was bred to be gentle. Wild rats are dangerous to touch, so if you see one, stay away!

I've heard of dog and cat allergies, but I've never heard of a rat allergy. Are rat allergies real?

 Yes! People can be allergic to any furry animal, but their allergy is actually not from the fur. People are allergic to what's on an animal's fur, like certain proteins, saliva, urine, or skin cells.

How do white blood cells know the difference between other white blood cells and invaders?

 Little protein labels tell the white blood cells which are our white blood cells and which are invaders. Then, they attack!

My friend is allergic to tree nuts, so we don't bring any to school. How do people know what they're allergic to?

 Doctors called allergists test you to see what causes a reaction, so you can avoid it!

What's the difference between a white blood cell and a T cell?

Actually, a T cell is a special type of white blood cell. T cells help the body protect itself from invaders. Some T cells attack and kill viruses and some T cells send instructions to the rest of your body.

Are there other types of cells besides white blood cells?

There sure are! We have tons of different cells, which all have important roles that keep our body working.

Thanks for the help, Professor Frizzle!

Keep the questions coming, students! Sneeze and thank you!

QUESTIONS and ACTIVITIES

1. If you could choose any class pet, what would it be? Draw a picture of the class pet of your dreams.

2. Carlos's immune system identified the Magic School Bus as an invader. What are some ways that his immune system tried to fight it off?

3. Look at the picture on page 68. How do you think Carlos feels about having to bring Ratney back to the shelter?

4. Tim and Jyoti use the 3-D printer to make an allergen grabber. What would you make in your 3-D printer?

5. When they walked past the garden, why did Wanda suspect that Carlos wasn't allergic to Ratney?